How Old is GRANDMA?

Antoinette Simmonds

Illustrated by Ian Dale

INOY
PRODUCTIONS

HOW OLD IS GRANDMA?
Published by INOT Productions

INOT
PRODUCTIONS

INOTproductions.com

Text © 2020 INOT Productions
Illustrations © 2020 Ian Dale

Library of Congress Control Number: 2020908632
ISBN (Hardcover) 978-0-578-63411-1
ISBN (Paperback) 978-1-7350295-2-8
eISBN 978-1-7350295-0-4

Printed in the United States of America
First Edition 2020

Dedication

I dedicate this book in memory of my dad, Houston, and mom, Roberta, who inspired me to pursue my dreams. My mom loved to sing, and my dad kept a watchful eye on all of us. Throughout the book, you will see a butterfly fluttering his wings. The butterfly represents my dad hovering over family and friends with words of encouragement and wisdom. You will also notice a bird that appears ready to imitate a song. The bird symbolizes my mom, who was an avid reader, a delightful storyteller, and a spontaneous, natural singer.

I also dedicate this book to my husband, Ken; daughters, Karla and Adrienne; my sister, Marcia; my aunt Madeline, aunt Pauline, family and friends here and abroad.

Finally, I extend special accolades to the characters of this book: Papa, our daughter-in-law, Trisha, our three grandsons, and an *exceptional thanks* to my son, Kendall, for his arduous work. Kendall has helped me bring my story to print over the last few years. You'll see more of this family's adventures in the next book, *Lizzy Has Big Feet*. Enjoy!

—Antoinette Simmonds

My name is Kendall. Luis is
my next-door neighbor.

We are both four years old and live
in Pleasant Town, California.

On sunny days, we love to play soccer.

When we were very small, we
watched our fathers play soccer.

And now, we play too!

I also have a younger brother,
named Kayson.

He likes to watch us run back and forth.

We laugh and have fun and
try to score a goal.

"Goal!" I shout.

"G-O-A-L!" shouts Luis. He stretches
out the word—loud and long,
letting each sound roll out of his
mouth. "G-O-O-O-A-A-A-L-L-L!"

We laugh and try again to score.

As we laugh and play, my mother calls to us.

"Kendall and Kayson! It's time to go to Grandma and Papa's house!"

"Luis, I have to go now," I say.

"But we can play again tomorrow."

"Why do you have to go?" Luis asks.

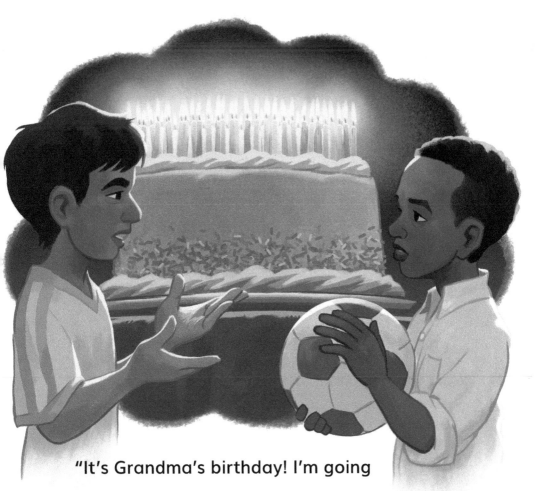

"It's Grandma's birthday! I'm going to put the candles on the cake!"

"How old is your Grandma?" Luis asks.

"I don't know," I say.

"Well, how many candles will you put on the cake?" Luis asks.

"Beats me! Maybe two thousand? No! Maybe a zillion?!"

"How old is your Grandma, Luis?" I ask.

"I don't know," Luis replies. "When we go fishing along the pier, we push Grandma in her wheelchair. She watches us catch fish. At home, we help Grandma bake cookies and cakes for us. After baking, she always says, '*Hora de la siesta!*— Nap time!' Then she takes a nap."

"Yeah, my Grandma plays soccer with us, and then she takes a nap too," I say.

"Kendall and Kayson, come on inside so we can go," says Mommy.

"Ok, Mommy." I wave to Luis. "We'll see you when we get back, Luis."

"Mommy, how old is Grandma?" I ask.

"Well, Kendall, you'll have to ask your dad," Mommy says.

I go find Daddy out by the car.

"Daddy, how old is Grandma?"

"That's a good question, Kendall.

You should ask Grandma when we see her."

Hmmm, I think. Kayson and I
are the only grandchildren, and
Grandma likes to run with us.

So maybe she's not a zillion after all.

"How many candles make a
zillion?" I ask Mommy.

"Well, I don't think you need a zillion
candles for Grandma's cake!"

"On my next birthday, I will put five
candles on my cake. And Kayson will get
two candles. Maybe I will get to fill up
Grandma's whole cake with candles!"

I can't wait to see Grandma.

Kayson and I like to visit our grandparents' house.

I always know their house is close when we turn on the corner and see the big, yellow house and tall palm trees.

When we go up to their door, I ring the bell and hide my face, so no one will see me.

Mommy uses her key to get in.

Daddy shouts, "Hi, Mom
and Dad, we're here!"

Papa shouts back, "Hello and welcome!"

He opens his arms and Kayson
and I run to him.

"Papa, where's Grandma?" I ask.

"Grandma is in the backyard," Papa says.

"She is getting ready to do her stretches."

"Stretches? I thought Grandma
was already tall!"

I go to the backyard to see
what Grandma is doing.

"Hi, Kendall!" Grandma smiles
and gives me a hug.

"I need your help in counting. Would you
like to do stretching exercises with me?"

"Yes, I can help!"

"Okay," says Grandma. "First, we
have to touch our toes ten times.
Can you count with me?"

"One, two, three," I say.

Grandma stops. "That's enough of that!" She reaches for the fan.

"But, Grandma, you didn't touch your toes!" I say.

"Oops! You are right, Kendall," she says.

"And Grandma, we only counted to three!"

"Right again, Kendall," says Grandma.

"Stretching is a lot of work. Phew!

Now it's time to take a

break," Grandma says.

"But I'm not tired," I say.

"Can we play soccer?"

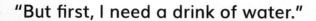

"Well, okay," says Grandma.

"But first, I need a drink of water."

My grandparents are one team.

Daddy and I are the other team.

Everyone says, "Okay, let's play!"

Mommy and Kayson sit on the side, watching.

The lawn chair is the goal. I kick the ball under the chair.

"GOAL!" I scream.

"Goal!" Papa shouts.

"Goal!" Daddy cheers.

"Goal!" Grandma yells.
She sits down in the chair.

Then Grandma says, "I remember when I use to run like this!" She moves her arms as fast as she can in her chair. She lifts her little legs off the ground.

Suddenly, something happens!

Grandma sits straight up and lets out a strange sound. "I-EEE-Yah!"

Her arms move faster and faster. She kicks the ball out from under the chair and starts running after it.

She runs around the field like a slow-motion tornado! She spins and twirls and makes a cloud of dust.

"Where's Grandma?" I ask.

"What happened to Grandma?"

As the dust settles, out comes Grandma.

She looks like a smashed marshmallow!

She wobbles like a duck, from side to side
toward the door.

"Grandma! Are you okay?" I ask.

The only thing we hear her say is, "I'm not hurt, but it's time for a nap!"

Suddenly, my baby brother claps. He wants a nap too.

We all say, "It's time for a break."

When Grandma wakes up
from her nap, I ask,

"Is it time to put the candles
on the cake, Grandma?"

"Yes, Kendall, the cake has cooled off.

We can decorate it now."

I ask, "How many candles do
you want on the cake?"

"Well, at my age, let's just put one candle in the middle of the cake," Grandma says.

"Only one candle, Grandma?"

I looked at Grandma and shouted in a loud voice, "GRANDMA IS OLD!"

"What?"
Daddy asks,
as he comes
into the kitchen.

"What?"
Papa asks,
as he sits
at the counter.

"Why do you
say that?"
Mommy asks.

Now that everyone is watching, I say it again, "GRANDMA IS OLD."

"Hmmm," Daddy says. "Grandma is my mother. Is that what makes her old?"

"No," I say.

"Grandma likes taking naps, is that what makes her old?" Mommy asks.

"Nope," I say.

"My teacher says that the word *grandma* means 'old.' So . . . *Grandma* IS 'old,'" I explain.

"Oh, I see!" Daddy smiles at Mommy and Papa. "It's the *name* 'grandma' that means old. Now I understand!"

"Well, clearly we need another name for Grandma that is not old!" Grandma laughs.

"Your name should be Nana," I say.

"*Nana.* I like that name. I feel younger already. Nana fits me just fine!" Nana says.

"Nana," I say, "can I put one candle on the cake?" Kayson says, "Me too!"

"Yes, Kendall and Kayson, I would like that," Nana says.

Can you read us a story, Nana?"

"Oh, yes!" says Nana, "That was my birthday wish!"

I go and find my favorite story.

I never do find out how old my grandmother is, but that's okay.

Not all grandmothers are the same.

Some are fast and
run, jump, and roll in
the grass to play.

Some grandmothers
are slower and
use a cane.

Other grandmothers
need a little help
in a special way.

But no matter what, if grandmas are
short or tall, fast or slow, young or old,
there is one thing I know for sure . . .

GRANDMA IS LOVE

Happy birthday, Nana!

CPSIA information can be obtained
at www.ICGtesting.com
Printed in the USA
BVHW020234130820
586307BV00015B/350